FRANCISCO

By Robert Maiorano

Illustrated by Rachel Isadora

MACMILLAN PUBLISHING CO., INC.
New York
COLLIER MACMILLAN PUBLISHERS
London

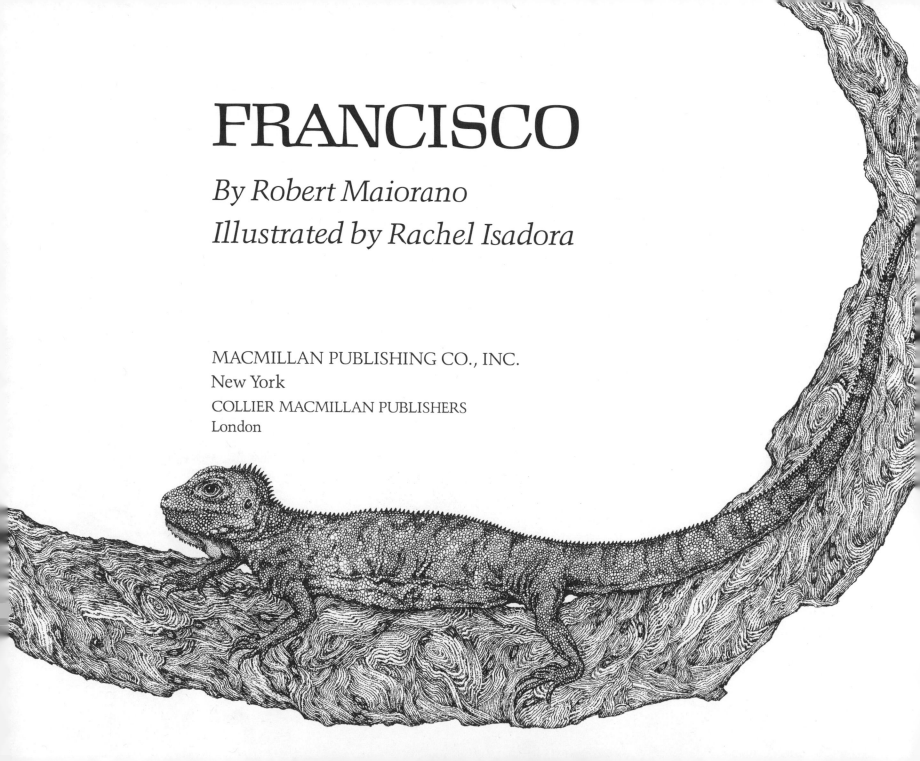

for
Hope · Bobby
Rita · Abraham
and Señor Moncion

Macmillan Publishing Co., Inc.
866 Third Avenue, New York, N.Y. 10022
Collier Macmillan Canada, Ltd.

Printed in the United States of America

10 9 8 7 6 5 4 3 2 1

LIBRARY OF CONGRESS CATALOGING IN PUBLICATION DATA

Maiorano, Robert.
   Francisco.
   SUMMARY: A young boy in the Dominican
Republic must provide food for his family while
his father is away.
   [1. Children in the Dominican Republic—
Fiction. 2. Dominican Republic—Fiction]
I. Isadora, Rachel. II. Title.
PZ7.M2783Fr [E] 78-4574 ISBN 0-02-762170-7

Dominican Republic
of
Hispaniola

Francisco lives near the mouth
of the Yuna River,
which comes from the mountains
of the Dominican Republic
and flows into the sea.

By the sea Francisco rides Duarté.

Francisco's father is a fisherman,
and he rides Duarté to the market
to sell his fish.

Most of the time there is enough fish to sell. But sometimes there is only enough to feed the family.

One day Francisco's father comes home
with his head down.
He tells his family
that their grandmother
is very sick.
   "I must go up the river
to take care of Grandmother Rosa.
I will be gone for three weeks."

He says to Francisco, "While I am gone,
you must take care of your mother, Gabriella,
Nina, Isabella and little Luís."

Francisco watches his father go as far as the turn in the river.

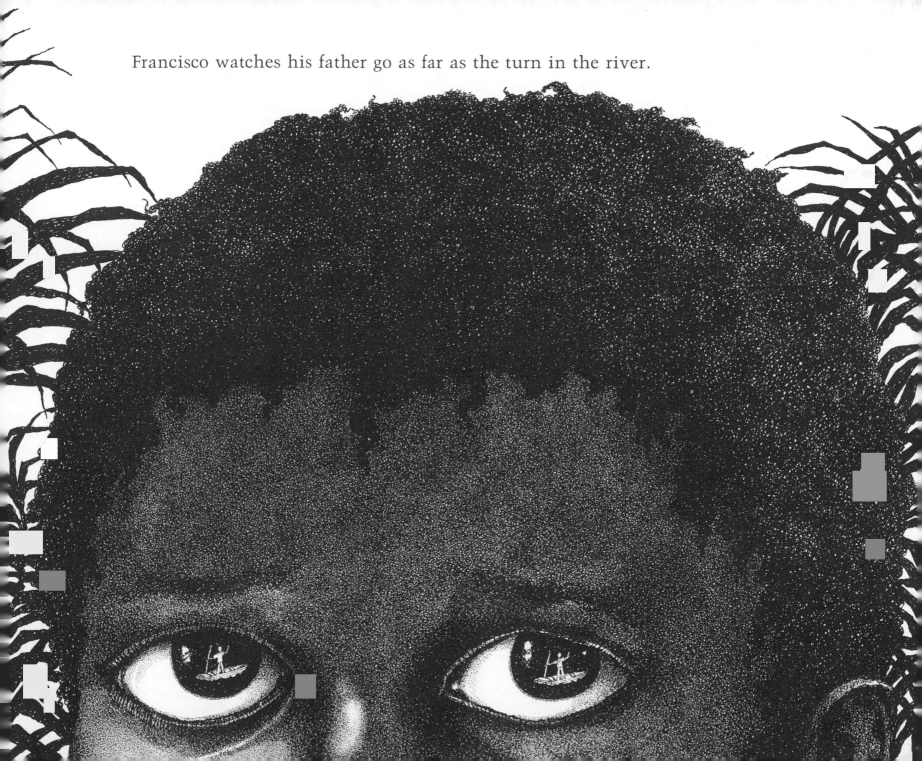

The next morning Francisco goes to the river
and fishes all day under the hot sun.

But he only catches one little fish.

At dinner Francisco's mother cuts the fish into six pieces.

After eating, Francisco sits by the river.

Early next morning he sets out for the beach with Duarté.
He fishes off a jetty, but the fish don't bite.

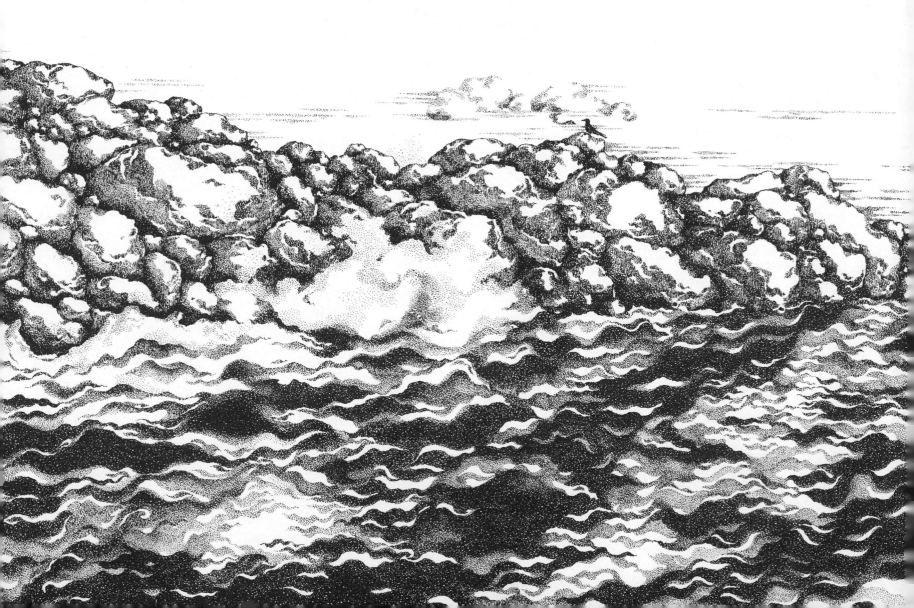

He walks along the beach
and looks for seashells
to sell to the tourists.
But most of the shells
are broken.

"OW!"

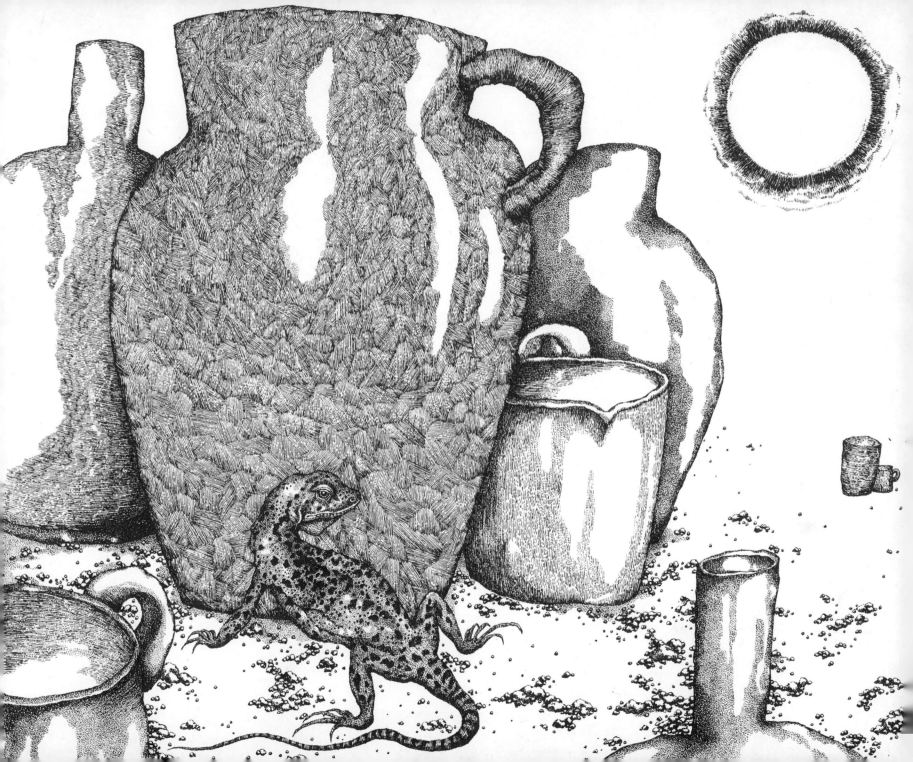

Later Francisco rides to the road where clay pots are
drying in the strong sun. "Can I help?" he asks.
"No," says the woman. "Maybe someday, when you are older."

Francisco walks away and sits under a coconut palm.
"What can we do?" he asks Duarté.

"Duarté!"

They ride to the part of the beach where all the tourists are.
Francisco points to Duarté, and the tourists understand.

He collects ten centavos for every donkey ride.

Now Francisco has found a way to get food for his family.